The Adventures of Maebh
The Warrior Queen

This story was adapted by author Ann Carroll
and illustrated by Derry Dillon

Published 2014
Poolbeg Press Ltd

123 Grange Hill, Baldoyle
Dublin 13, Ireland

Text © Poolbeg Press Ltd 2014

A catalogue record for this book is available from the British Library.

ISBN 978 1 78199 998 1

Cover design and illustrations by Derry Dillon
Printed by GPS Colour Graphics Ltd, Alexander Road, Belfast BT6 9HP

This book belongs to

- -

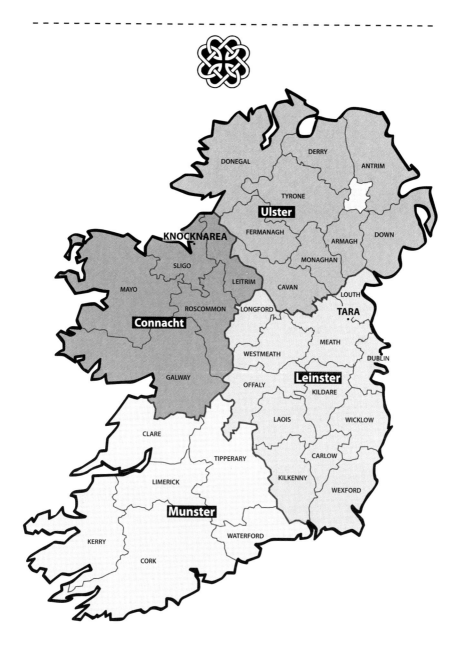

Also in the Nutshell series

The Children of Lir
How Cúchulainn Got His Name
The Story of Saint Patrick
The Salmon of Knowledge
The Story of the Giant's Causeway
The Story of Newgrange
Granuaile the Pirate Queen
Oisín and Tír na nÓg
The Story of Brian Boru
Deirdre of the Sorrows
Heroes of the Red Branch Knights
The Adventures of the Fianna

A Terrible Torment

One day long ago, Eochaidh Feidleach, the High King of Ireland, had nothing to do, so he started thinking about his daughter, Maebh. She was an awful worry to him and soon he began to groan: "What will I do with her? She's young and beautiful and I love her dearly, but she's a terrible torment. She never does a thing I ask. When she doesn't get her own way she turns quite nasty. And then if I say a word she bites my head off! That's no way to treat a father, never mind a High King."

Just then a messenger arrived from Conor Mac Nessa, the King of Ulster, and told Eochaidh: "My King has a great palace at Eamhain Macha. He has lots of gold. His army of Red Branch Knights is the best in the world. His nephew Cúchulainn is the best warrior in the world. The best musicians and storytellers are in his court and he gives the best feasts!"

"So?" Eochaidh said, irritated by these Best-Boasts.

"So, the one thing he hasn't got on his Best-List is a wife. He knows that your daughter, Maebh, is the fairest in the land and he wants to marry her."

Eochaidh perked up no end, but didn't want to appear too enthusiastic. "I will consider his request," he said.

"Conor wants three things in a wife," added the messenger. "She must think the world of him, do his bidding and look after him well. In other words, she must be The Best!"

Eochaidh drew himself up. "That's no problem for Maebh! I have given his proposal consideration and to show my great respect I'll allow him to marry Maebh immediately."

In no time at all the wedding took place at Tara. As the couple set off on the journey to Eamhain Macha, the High King waved them off. As soon as they were out of sight he jigged for joy all around the palace and was jolly with everyone for days.

The Worst Wife in the World

Within a year Maebh had a son, Glaisne. But she hated her husband.

"Conor is so full of his own importance," she thought. "And so bossy and bad-tempered. And he's always thinking up ways to make me miserable."

One day she told him: "I know you wanted
to add me to your Best-List and that's the only
reason you married me. I'm just a trophy."

"A trophy? You're a disaster!" Conor said.
"You're on my Worst of the Worst List! You
must be the Worst Wife in the World!"

And so, highly insulted, Maebh left Eamhain
Macha and returned to her father.

Eochaidh wasn't a bit happy. "Conor must be furious," he thought, "for it's obvious she didn't do his bidding. She certainly didn't think the world of him and she definitely didn't look after him! He'll blame me."

He knew Conor would make a powerful enemy and so arranged for Eithne, another daughter of his, to marry him.

Maebh's Revenge

Soon Eithne was expecting a baby and Conor was very happy as this wife fulfilled all his wishes.

But Maebh couldn't stand the thought of Conor's happiness and saw her sister as disloyal. "How could she marry a man who treated me so badly? She knows I loathe him."

Maebh never forgave anyone she thought had wronged her and she had Eithne murdered, thinking to destroy the child as well, but the baby was delivered after his mother's death and was called Furbaide.

Eithne's death caused a lot of upset in Tara and in Ulster. But instead of punishing Maebh (for at heart he was truly fond of her) her father decided to make her Queen of Connacht.

At least that would keep her far away from Tara and give him a calmer life.

Two More Husbands

Connacht already had a king, Tinni Mac Conri, but he was easily displaced, not having much of an army. However, he was a very handsome man and Maebh married him, and for a while things went well and there was peace in the land.

Then one day Maebh started thinking about her marriage. "I want three things from a husband," she mused. "He must be generous, without fear and have no jealousy." Then she thought about Tinni. "He's generous enough and brave enough, but he's very jealous!"

The chief of Maebh's bodyguard was a young, handsome warrior, Ailill Mac Máta. He thought the world of Maebh and couldn't hide his love. Tinni saw this and challenged Ailill to armed combat. But after a fierce fight it was Tinni who was slain.

Ailill, the conquerer, won not only the fight but also Maebh, and when they married he became King of Connacht and they had seven sons and one daughter, Findebar.

The Seven Maines

However, Maebh still hated her first husband, Conor Mac Nessa, and reared her sons to hate him too. One day she asked the court druid, "How will Conor die?"

Druids were wise men with magical powers and could tell the future. They could also be quite tricky with their answers.

"Conor will be killed by a man called Maine," this druid replied.

"Right!" Maebh said. "Then I will rename all of my sons. Starting with the first-born, they will be called:

Father's Maine

Mother's Maine

Maine the Swift

Maine the Silent

Maine the Dutiful

Sweet-talking Maine

And finally: Maine Beyond Description.

With seven Maines the chances are good one of them will kill Conor!"

And indeed, Maine the Swift did slay a man called Conor, but he was not Conor Mac Nessa.

Jealousy, Arguments and the Great White Bull

It happened that Fergus Mac Roich, a mighty Ulster warrior, fell out with Conor and came to Connacht. Maebh welcomed him to her court. He was brave and daring and soon in love with the Queen.

They were always together and Ailill was raging. He brooded, "If Maebh knows I'm jealous, I'll lose her. I could challenge Fergus to combat, but he is an excellent fighter and I could lose my wife and my life! I'll just have to bide my time."

But he and Maebh began to argue over everything except Fergus.

One day Ailill boasted, "I'm richer than you. I've more of everything than you. That makes me better than you!"

"You're definitely not richer than me!" Maebh was furious. "Sure you were only a bodyguard till I married you. You couldn't have more than I have."

"Yes, I could!"

"No, you couldn't!"

By now they were roaring.

Then they hit on a brilliant idea: "Let's prove who is the richest. Let's compare everything we own!"

So they compared cutlery, goblets, fine wines, gold, ornaments, clothes, jewellery, weapons and chariots. All were of equal value.

Next came horses, hounds, sheep and cattle and anything else they owned. Again, there was no difference in worth.

"Now!" said Maebh. "That's everything we have and you're NOT richer than me."

"I am so," said Ailill. "For I've kept the best till last – my great white bull, Finnbennach. He's worth a fortune and you, my dear, have nothing to match him!"

War!

Well, Maebh was beside herself with rage. She sent messengers to every part of Ireland to find a bull that would outclass Finnbennach. At last a mighty brown bull was found in Ulster at Cooley.

Maebh made a generous offer for the animal and the owner agreed to sell, but then he overheard her messengers say she'd have used force if he'd refused. He was so annoyed he decided to keep the bull and throw out the messengers.

So Maebh went to war. She gathered a great army and, with Fergus by her side, she marched on Ulster.

Conor's army, the Red Branch Knights, was under a sleeping spell. The one warrior left awake was Cúchulainn, Conor's nephew. He was the greatest fighter ever and single-handedly defended Ulster, killing hundreds of the enemy, most of them in single combat at a ford in the river. This stand-off lasted for months.

Fergus Mac Roich refused to fight Cúchulainn to the death because he was his godson. But a great Connacht warrior, Ferdia, a boyhood friend of Cúchulainn's, was goaded into combat by Maebh.

In the bloody fight that followed, both young men met their deaths. But by then the Red Branch Knights had woken and they battled fiercely till Connacht was beaten.

Nevertheless, Maebh managed to capture the Brown Bull of Cooley and take him home, where he turned at once on Finnbennach, killed him and wandered off home to Ulster.

So the death of Cúchulainn and Ferdia and of all the brave young warriors was for nothing.

The End of Fergus and Ailill

Ailill never got over his jealousy. One day, spying on Maebh and Fergus in the woods, the king saw his chance. He got a blind archer to fire an arrow, telling him the target was a deer. The archer aimed straight and true and Fergus was killed.

But the Queen found out Ailill was responsible and, never the forgiving type, she had her husband killed.

The Past Catches Up

Maebh's violent past came looking for her. Furbaide, the son of her sister, Eithne, had been reared on the story of his mother's murder. Now he was grown-up and sought revenge.

Furbaid knew his aunt bathed each day in a certain pool in Sligo. He spied on her from a safe hiding place. When she was gone he measured the distance to Maebh's spot in the pool.

"Now!" he said. "I will go away and practise with my sling till I can hit a target that distance away."

When Furbaid was absolutely accurate he came back to his hiding place. He fitted a round of hard cheese onto his sling, for it was light enough to travel the distance and lethal enough to kill.

He fired and Maebh was killed instantly.

It is said that the great queen is buried, standing, under the cairn of stones at Knocknarea in Sligo. She faces Ulster, the kingdom of her greatest enemy and first husband, Conor.

Even in death Maebh does not forget or forgive.

The End

Word Sounds

(Opinions may differ regarding pronunciation)

Words	Sounds
Maebh	Maeve
Eochaid	Ucky
Feidleach	Fed-lock
Furbaide	Forbid-eh
Tinni	Tinny
Mac Conri	Mock-on-ree
Ailill	Al-ill
Mac Máta	Mock Mawta
Mac Roich	Mock Roe-ick
Finnbennach	Fin-ben-ock

Also available from the IN A NUTSHELL series

All you need to know about Ireland's best loved stories in a nutshell